SHADOWS
THINGS THAT GO BUMP

DANIEL PERRY

SHADOWS

© 2014 Daniel Perry

All Rights Reserved

ISBN: 1496022890
ISBN13: 978-1496022899

DANIEL PERRY

The characters and situations depicted in this work are fictional. Any resemblance to persons living or deceased is purely coincidental and in no way intended by the author.

This work may not be copied or stored in any manner except for this original, including electronic storage without prior consent of the author.

SHADOWS

BOOKS BY DANIEL PERRY

CHILDREN'S
The Case of the Missing Shoes

NON-FICTION
Safe and Sound

Black Belt Economics

Modern Tournament Production

SHORT STORIES
Shadows

Coven Rule

FICTION (Novel)
The Chimera Alpha Project

SHADOWS

For Christian and Caedmon.
You are my inspiration
to continue to reinvent myself
and push forward.

<u>1</u>

Clairmore Manor has been my home for as long as I can remember. It is an expansive estate nestled in the foothills of the great Smokey Mountains of North Carolina.

I spend my days going place to place collecting as much information as I can. Researching, because I know one day in the future I will be needed and I plan to be well armed with as much data as possible to help the good side prevail. My name is Kevin Hall.

My nights are spent at the Manor. Not by choice mind you, but something always draws me back at dark. I live here with a family. Greg, the head of the household, is a general practice physician. His hours are pretty well set with a thriving practice that allows for a regular schedule. Alyse is a stay at home mom who home schools their two children, Robert, 9 and Stacey, 12.

The children and the family pet, Charlie, (A mutt that was rescued from a horrible future at the local animal shelter.) seem to know something is a little different here. They are sensitive to the subtle changes that people like me create. The adults, however, go about their daily business as if there is nothing in the entire world to worry about or be frightened of.

They are wrong. There are things I have discovered, I would not have believed myself. You know the stories we all hear when we are children about monsters? Well, it turns out they are all true. These things are hidden from the world and exist on their own plane with rules put in place by those who understand the devastation such knowledge would cause.

Just like anything else, there is a flip side. There are always those who do not like to follow the rules. Just like some in the human world, they have other agendas that are not in the best interest of all but rather self-serving in nature.

I chose a side and vowed to help fight for what is right in order to keep everyone safe and blissfully unaware of what is actually out there in the world.

I have discovered all of this not because I am smart and figured it out. In fact, it was only because of a need I have. I need to some-how, be useful, even in the form I am in.

I am one of the monsters I spoke of before. I have not been alive as you would know it for just over a year.

I guess if it had to be termed, I am a ghost. I prefer spirit but it is what it is. I have found that in my world, those who meet with violent death and continue to have a purpose to fulfill, become trapped on this earth.

Many of the things you have heard about ghosts are true. The living, humans, are not able to see or hear me unless I want them to. However, there are para-beings with other talents who can see spirits.

I am able to move small objects, pass through walls and even sense when there are others of my kind around.

From everything I have learned, ghosts are kind of neutral in all the battles that are ongoing in this alternate world of monsters.

There are werewolves and vampires who have hated each other for centuries. No one really knows the origin of this rivalry but it is severe. Witches and the undead have been on-again-off-again.

The thing is, they have been able to co-exist in the human world and with the exception of rumor and legend, stay hidden from the populous for centuries.

2

I am the only spirit who haunts the manor. This made the first part of my time very difficult. I went through the first several months in a state of denial. I just could not believe I was dead. It is frustrating to attempt to go about your daily routine without being able to truly accomplish any tasks.

As I settled on what I was, I had some fun playing a few minor pranks, eavesdropping and exploring any new found talents.

While I was alive I worked as a musician of sorts. I spent my days writing cute little jingles for products. I am sure you have heard some of them so much they are stuck in your brain for all eternity. It paid well and offered me the ability to live a care free lifestyle.

One night during my thirty-fifth year a man came to my door. He was very tan with shoulder length brown hair and a stubble filled face. He was covered in dark red blood and pleaded with me through the door to help him.

He said he had been attacked along the roadway and the people who had done this had taken his car and wallet before leaving him for dead.

Of course I brought him inside and called the police. They told me they would send an ambulance and officer.

I cleaned the man up and began to look at his wounds. They were deep and many of them appeared as though a knife blade had slashed at his flesh over and over.

He barely winced when I cleaned them as though he felt very little pain. I knew it would take the Emergency Medical Services (EMS) at least half an hour to arrive so after checking for active bleeding I told the stranger I was going to make some tea and he should just stay still until they arrived.

When I returned from the kitchen the man was gone and there in my living room was the largest dog I had ever seen.

His fur was the same color brown as the stranger's hair and they shared the same eyes. Before I could even start to process any of this, the beast was on me.

In one leap he had knocked me to the ground and had pinned me beneath his mass. His mouth on my neck, the two and a half inch fangs had buried into my throat. He did not tear at the flesh but rather applied a vice-like pressure that effectively cut my airway off. When I began to kick and squirm in panic, he sat down on my thighs to keep me still. I lost consciousness in just about thirty seconds.

I woke, or at least I thought I was awake and saw the tail of the animal disappear out the door I had left open earlier. I ran after him. I was amazed I was able to keep pace for a little while. He stayed too far in front of me to catch yet close enough to be in sight. I felt like I was running effortlessly. I did not get winded and I did not slow my pace. This went on I know for a few hours then as if he was done with the game, he vanished into the night.

It was a long walk back to the house and by this time, I had forgotten about the EMS. When I returned home, I went about my business as usual.

It would be a few weeks before I realized that the beast had taken my life that night. While my spirit was on a chase I know now to be a distraction, the authorities had entered my home, discovered and removed my body. That is why I did not know I was dead. I never saw my own body as many do.

The first I actually knew something might be wrong was when the realtor came and placed the house up for sale. I approached him as he made his way about making sure the place was in good enough shape to show to prospective buyers. He was not able to hear or see me. No matter what I tried I could not get him to recognize the fact I was there.

Knowing this was a problem and something strange was happening, I rode along as he drove back into town.

While in town I decided to nose around and see if I could come across any information. At the library I was able to find the newspaper obituary of my death.

They had listed it as a tragic accident. Noting my pet dog, (whatever!), had attacked and killed me and then ran away and was not able to be found. Since there was no next of kin, I was buried in the town cemetery. I remember wondering how in hell they could get it so completely wrong.

I spent the rest of the afternoon wandering around the library. I was listening to various conversations I had no business hearing. There was someone cheating on taxes, and yet another planning to leave her husband. It was getting late and I was just starting to think about how I was going to get myself back home. Then without another thought I was back in the manor on the very spot where I had met my demise.

I tried to go out the front door and found myself back on my death spot. Trying the back door yielded the same result. I was trapped in the house.

Over time, I learned one of the unwritten rules of being a ghost is you are returned to where you were killed at dusk and must remain there until dawn. This is why all of the reports of hauntings and ghost sightings happen at night. That is when we are at home.

3

The first family to move into the manor after my death was a husband and wife. They were easy. I would do simple things like open drawers and cabinets, pull covers off of them in the night, and knock over an occasional item. They only stayed about two weeks. They left in a hurry and many of their items still remain in the attic and basement areas of the manor.

This show of force brought some unwanted attention to the house. I had to endure the ghost hunters and paranormal experts as they probed and filmed and implemented all sorts of gadgets to find me.

I decided I did not like or want this attention so I kept to myself. They eventually gave up.

All the toys they used, the electro-magnetic imagers and infrared scanners, low frequency recorders, are just a hoax. I suppose it helps to sale the service and television shows. Fact of the matter is if a spirit does not want you to know they are there, you will never know it.

The place stayed empty for some time and I figured out I could leave during the daytime hours. I went to the gravesite where I had been buried. It was a little eerie but I needed to see it.

That is where I encountered a few more like me. I was amazed there were actually people who had been killed in the cemetery.

One was an elderly man named Charles. He had been killed here in 1928 in a dispute over a gambling debt. Debbie was the other who had been haunting the grounds since 1976 after a group of boys drove her here, attacked and killed her.

Both had been buried in fresh graves so it would appear nothing had been disturbed.

These were good people and good spirits. I was lucky in the fact since they had been in this form for much longer than I, they could teach me and give me information I would not have otherwise.

They filled me in on things like passing through objects and how the things and stories we knew as legend, were true.

There are different types of spirits, I learned. Some had a giving personality in the living world, they were like us. They are just trying to make some sense out of the cards they were given to play. Others, who were evil, tended to remain so in the afterlife. This accounted for poltergeist and possessions.

Humans can and have been killed by ghosts. It is usually written off as an accident or suicide but there are other forces involved many times.

I discovered there is only one way to keep spirits in line and following the rules. Witches are the only supernatural power who can control spirits. I guess I shouldn't have been surprised. If ghosts are real why wouldn't witches be as well?

Many of them live right alongside ordinary humans.

They are mediums, psychics, and apothecary owners. They will set themselves up in a profession the general public sees as odd so as not to bring attention to the fact they are real. Witches are female and warlocks are male. There are covens, supporting the family structure for them much as werewolves have packs and vampires, colonies.

It was difficult for me to absorb this information at first. I did not want to believe any of it. Yet here I was, a ghost talking with other ghosts in the middle of a cemetery, after being taken from the living world by a werewolf. So what could be further fetched then that.

<u>4</u>

Charles and Debbie invited me to my first meeting. I couldn't help but laugh a little about how organized this all felt. It was like I was in AA or something and my sponsors wanted to get me to open up in my first group session.

"Hello, my name is Kevin and I'm a ghost."

The meeting took place outside in a large open area surrounded by woods on the outskirts of town. It was early in the morning and not under the moon like you may have heard. The spirits attending these things are forced back to their haunts at night so it has to be held during the daylight hours.

There were four spirits, nine witches, and one warlock in attendance. It was absolutely insane. The meeting was called to order. They read old business and new business. Talked a little about the next get together then asked about any new members.

It felt like an Elks club meeting or something.

Charles introduced me to the group and I told the group my story about how I had been killed by a werewolf and now I haunted Clairmore Manor.

The woman leading the group introduced herself as Mary Martin. She said since I was a new member they would cover some of the basics.

"Besides" she said, "everyone could use a refresher."

She explained that there are things in this world that lie beyond what a human can comprehend. There are some good and some bad but all existed for centuries. The stories about the boogie man are true to some extent and if it were not for rules, there would be chaos.

The number one rule of all para-beings is that humans are not to be harmed.

"Now I know you were killed by a wolf. The fact is, just like the human world, we have our problems. You most likely were attacked by a stray (a wolf that lives outside of the pack rule). He will be caught and he will be punished." She went on to say the wolves take care of their own affairs.

The alpha manages the pack and for the most part does a fantastic job.

"The second rule is you are to leave no trace. We do not do anything or create anything that could leave a trail or make the humans believe we are real. If it ever came to fruition this alternate world was true, the war and bloodshed would be great and most likely end with the extermination of all humans."

For Ghosts, there was a third rule. We have to protect our haunts at all costs. If something were to happen to the location where we had met our demise, we would become roaming spirits and that is not allowed. Roaming spirits are destroyed to prevent havoc.

I asked how many types of para-beings there were. The answer was five. There are ghosts, witches, werewolves, vampires, and the un-dead, or as some call them, zombies.

Ghosts are a natural occurrence and directly related to violent death. Vampires, werewolves and zombies have a type of mutated parvovirus and witches are born into witchcraft families, trained from birth to use their special skill sets.

Each group has to be looked at separately. Although there is currently a truce between everyone it has not always been so.

Currently each group takes care of their own house, so to speak, with the exception of spirits that are monitored by the covens and the wolves who help keep zombie population under control which is a task she assured me was absolutely a needed service.

We have enjoyed a peace for many years but there is something lately that does not feel right.

There is a rift taking place and it seems to be starting with the spirit world. Mary Martin told me if I had any information that may be of use to please contact her. She provided her address and went back to call the meeting back to order.

The members of the coven formed a circle and began to chant.

I had not felt anything as far as sensation since my death. However, when they began I could tell the wind had picked up and a chill began to fill the air. It was empowering. As if I could smell the earth and somehow I was genetically programmed and connected to this magic.

5

When I returned to the Manor something felt odd. Out of place even. Like when you know there is a difference from what is normal and cannot put your finger on exactly what it is.

I had a lot on my mind after the information I had received and I chalked the feeling up to that.

There was no one home and as it was early in the evening, I figured they must have gone to dinner.

If I could pinpoint something I missed about being alive the most, it would be eating.

The aroma of a good meal combined with the tastes and textures. There is so much joy in that.

Something caught my eye just for a second on the landing at the top of the stairs. It appeared as a gray shadow and from what I could tell had no particular form. It was more liquid in nature and even more, it was moving. I quickly moved toward the form.

As I approached the object dissipated. Just as if it were never really there. I am not sure if a dead man's eyes can play tricks. I know something was there. I looked for a source of light. Something that could have cast a shadow in the location but there was no trace of anything.

The front door opened and the family entered. They seemed to be in an overly good mood, laughing and picking at each other as families do.

Alyse went to the kitchen and started a pot of coffee. I remember wishing I could smell it. Greg started a fire in the fireplace. It was a massive structure that had been hand laid with stone. It had a mantel that was a foot thick. It had been carved from a solid piece of oak. It was always one of my favorite aspects of the house.

The kids went outside to bring Charlie in. He immediately ran to the top of the stairs and began to bark at the wall where the shadow had been. Greg quickly called him down and scolded him for his behavior. I knew there was something more to it. Just like the way a dog can hear higher pitches than humans, they also have a way of knowing when there is a presence.

A loud metallic clang echoed in the house when the flu of the fireplace had slammed closed on its own sending billows of thick smoke into the living area. Unseen by the living eyes, the smoke began to cling to two shapes sitting on the hearth. Gray shadows who wanted me to know they were there.

Charlie began to bark. Greg called him down once more and went to the fireplace to re-open the flu. After he accomplished the task scratching his head wondering how it had occurred, I went over and sat between the two gray shadows. There was no solid form to be seen even close up. The shadows seemed to be fluid and changed shape often. I was a little startled when one began to speak.

"My name is Kent Sanders", he said. "My wife Sarah is the other form you are seeing."

"What the hell are you doing in my house" I asked abruptly.

"Please let me explain, we mean no harm". I nodded in response as a gesture for him to continue.

"My wife and I had been killed by a wolf in our home about two years ago. Like you, we sought advice and help from others and things seemed to be going well.

Three nights ago, the same stray came back in his human form and destroyed our house. As I am sure you have discovered by now, without our house we became wandering spirits. That is why we appear the way we do. Only gray shadows with no true form."

He went on to tell me this was done on purpose and is happening all over. For some unknown reason the strays are trying to eliminate the ghosts. It is some kind of uprising or something.

He continued. "We are now running to keep the coven from banishing us to a limbo and at the same time attempting to recruit for our cause."

"What is it you want from me?" I questioned.

"We need a place to stay, somewhere no one will think to look for us. We can help you too. The stray that murdered you will most likely come back to destroy your haunt as well. We can help you take a stand and protect this house."

"Tell me more about what is going on."

Kent, or at least his shadow began to fill me in on what he knew. There were three kinds of wandering spirits. The Grays are the nonviolent ghosts of people like me who have lost their haunt and are forced to roam. The Blacks are more mischievous and tend to haunt places that do not belong to them.

They are the ones you hear about in all the ghost stories people tell. Then there are Reds. These are spirits that are controlled by evil. They are the mercenaries for the para-beings that do just about anything for anybody in exchange for protection from the coven.

The Strays have banded together to create a bastardized pack of their own and are now eliminating gray and black spirits while recruiting the reds.

Mary Martin was correct. There is something bad happening in this para-being world as she called it and I am right in the middle. I agreed that Kent and Sarah could stay. We would take a stand. The wolves would not get my house. Not if there was anything I could do about it.

6

As the days ticked by, we took turns guarding the property and not ever leaving it unattended. On the third day I was on patrol when a knock came at the door.

When Alyse answered, it was Mary. She was pretending to be a salesperson for products such as soaps and bath oils. After her pitch was politely turned down she turned and looked at me.

"We need to talk" she said. "Meet me in the clearing in an hour."

I did as I was told and after explaining to my guests, I headed to the clearing. Mary was already there and began to tell me a story.

She said that although werewolves are very real, much of what I heard about them in my lifetime was false.

The moon it seems has very little to do with them. Sometimes when they are fairly new to being a wolf, the atmospheric changes can trigger an instant transformation. For the most part wolves can change at will. It is traumatic and painful each time and most will only change when absolutely no other choice remains. High stress levels both physical and emotional can also trigger this.

They are extremely strong even in their human form. They do age but at a much slower rate than humans. A werewolf will live approximately four human lifetimes.

The most important thing is they can be killed. She said, "The stories about cutting off their heads or needing silver bullets to dispatch a werewolf, is all crap. They have all the same vulnerabilities as a human. It may just take a little more effort due to their strength."

She told me she wanted to educate me because she knew about my guests and the trouble that was coming my way. She said if the coven interfered at this point it could start a full out war and no one is prepared for that yet.

"Why are you not controlling my guests?"

"We are picking our battles right now Kevin. We know that reds are being recruited. We have to watch and wait for more information before we act. You have the right to defend your haunt and we wish you the best of luck in doing so."

She said she would be in touch. With that, we parted ways and I returned to the Manor to fill in my new allies.

<u>7</u>

It was just a few more days before the wolf approached my house. We watched as he walked up the drive rubbing blood from a plastic bag he was holding onto his head and face. He was tearing holes in his shirt as he rang the bell.

Greg was the one to answer this time. "I've been attacked." The wolf spat out in an Oscar winning performance. "Can you please help me?"

Greg helped him to the couch and told him to stay still while he went to get the first aid kit. He left the room and the wolf spoke.

"I know you are here. I will kill this family and destroy this house so sit back and enjoy the show."

Kent and Sarah pushed passed me.

"It is important that you stay clean." he said. I was not sure what he was trying to say at the time but later would understand. The wolf began his transformation. It was quick, not like in the movies. More of a morphing, it left him with the physical appearance of a large wolf. I guess I was expecting the half-wolf half-monster that is always portrayed.

He turned and looked directly at me. In human form they can only sense sprits are present but as a wolf, he could see me.

"Why are you doing this to us?" I screamed at the beast. He was no longer able to answer. In the form he had taken he could only grunt and snarl.

Distracted by my presence, the animal never saw the first blow coming. Kent had used the fireplace poker to impale the animal through his back. It must have missed his heart because after a brief yelp he turned and snapped at the fluid shadow that was on him. Kent's form split in half and rejoined itself in mid-air.

The kerosene lamp from the mantle was being manipulated by Sarah. She brought it down hard on the stray's skull, spilling the contents that quickly soaked into the thick brown fur.

I could hear Greg returning and I quickly found his path and closed and locked the door in front of him in a hope to stall his discovery of the fight that was playing out in his living area.

I returned in time to see a burning log from the fireplace drop from the air above and land on the wolf. The kerosene immediately burst into flames and the beast dropped to the floor screaming in pain.

Greg had heard the noise and kicked through the door. Seeing the fire in the middle of the floor he grabbed a blanket and smothered the flames. He had managed to keep the house from being badly damaged but thankfully was too late to save the wolf. It was over. We had won.

After the police arrived, Greg was informed about the dog attacks that had been discovered and was told how lucky he was an accident had taken the animal before he and his family became the next victims.

Greg thanked the authorities and they removed the carcass from the house. (Another wolf fact I did not know was if they die a wolf, they stay a wolf.)

A rug was used to cover the spot where the flames had scarred the hardwood floor. I turned to face the forms of Kent and Sarah. Their gray shadows had darkened. No longer were they innocent. Still homeless, the black shadows faded as they passed through the wall.

The fight had been won but at what cost. I knew somehow this was far from over. But, for now I was safe, the family was safe and my haunting continues.

COVEN RULE

Things that go Bump

Daniel Perry

THE STORY CONTINUES

SPRING 2014

Made in the USA
Columbia, SC
01 February 2020